T0082564

Dimension:
UNKNOWN

The unexplained...

D. J. BOUILLION

authorHOUSE®

AuthorHouse™
1663 Liberty Drive
Bloomington, IN 47403
www.authorhouse.com
Phone: 1 (800) 839-8640

Published by AuthorHouse 05/22/2017

ISBN: 978-1-5246-9376-3 (sc)
ISBN: 978-1-5246-9375-6 (e)

CONTENTS

THE PAINTED BUNTING

Awakened by an alarm so common to his ear Chad reached, desperately, to turn off the piercing sound of his alarm clock. He returned snuggled back to his long, restful spot to recapture that slumberous feeling. What seemed for a moment, the beginning of a monotonous and most uneventful day in the life of a twelve year old, was actually, the start of an adventure he could only dream of, or even live it.

It was Thursday morning and, as usual, he heard his ever-concerned mother calling his name from the kitchen below. "Breakfast is ready, Chad."

It was a sudden awakening again, even though the last alarm had sounded just a few minutes earlier.

Chad could not, if he wanted, escape the aroma of a good home-cooked meal and surely not the recognizable sounds of kitchen clatter. It was a sound that always encouraged him to get out of bed and begin his day but this morning seemed a little different. The morning possessed him and held him tightly. It seemed to paralyze his every move.

"I'll be there in a minute," Chad, hesitantly, responded. He felt the need to quietly lay there to capture a little more rest before breakfast.

As he gazed around his cluttered room, he curiously focused his sleepy eyes toward the windowsill. The sudden, clean-swept morning breeze gently lifted the curtains as to give a sign of life outside. Chad, patiently and willingly, allowed for one of nature's most carefree creatures to appear. This bird, of beautiful colors, was enticing to witness.

He was not one who was readily familiar with naming nature's own but he, undoubtedly, knew that this bird was a Painted Bunting. This flying array of colors was one of many that perch so peacefully on branches extending gracefully from the tall, oak trees as a way of guarding and guiding its fate. Chad gave this wonder of the sky a chance to check out a new, uncertain adventure.

Chad seemed so focused on his welcomed friend that he felt a strong, magnetic urge to take its place for a glimpse of the open skies with only a second by second worry of his own path. He carefully dictated every move not to create a sudden fear or surprise for his visitor.

"What a life!" Chad said quietly to himself.

Another abrupt call from his mother prompted a quick getaway for his morning, feathered friend. This was a very disappointed moment for him. He courageously retreated back to reality. He quickly got ready for breakfast and finished his morning ritual before his walk to Central Middle School.

His usual walk to school was different that morning. Gazing at the blue skies above, Chad slipped into an imaginative pattern of in-depth and serious daydreaming. The serene surroundings added to the picturesque view he created for himself. Again, he wished he was free as a bird and that he could explore the never-ending skies.

As always, Chad faithfully traveled the same semi-winding road to school. Time lapsed quickly while his thoughts engulfed his every step. He arrived just minutes to spare as he heard the sounds of the typical campus clatter.

Chad's unusually late arrival was quite evident to his closest friend. It was then that the sound of a three-second bell reminded all students that learning was just moments away. John, his best friend since Kindergarten, was eager to say good morning and was, indeed, curious to why he was late.

"Where were you Chad? Did you get lost?" John asked with a sarcastic tone in his voice.

"No. I just had a few chores to do before I left home this morning," Chad said with a serious grin on his face.

They both proceeded to the hallway lockers for a quick gathering of books for their first hour class.

The subject taught first hour was Life Science with Mr. Freeman. He was a well-liked teacher and very knowledgeable. Mr. Freeman was very committed to his daily lessons and wanted everyone's attention all the time. He treasured every scientific moment and struggled with the faintest idea that any student would be preoccupied with anything else. He knew; however, that Science was not always the main thought of a middle school student, especially first period of the morning. Nevertheless, Mr. Freeman wasted no time in beginning the lesson for the day. Chad, on the other hand, was still intrigued with his visit by the Painted Bunting.

The lesson seemed to drag-on as every minute slowly ticked away and it was time for the next class. This class would not be any different. It was Social Studies and Ms. Skyler was also demanding of her students' attention in class. Chad's indelible thoughts of his early morning visit kept him in a daze. He pondered relentlessly on one thing and only one thing, that being the Painted Bunting.

Recess was on everyone's mind, especially Chad. That time eventually arrived. The class ended as always with a reading assignment with questions to follow. Chad did not even take time to write the assignment as he hurriedly left the room. The slowness of time was agonizing to him.

Recess at Central gave just enough time to take care of the usual needs and a casual encounter with friends. The hallway filled with many loud voices and the clanging of lockers. Chad wanted to isolate himself from the crowd but it became difficult as his friends chatted around him.

Chad, of course, was not his normal self as well-noted by his friends. "Chad, what is wrong?" asked Jason, another very close friend.

"Nothing at all; I'm just feeling a little bit tired today," he hesitantly responded to avoid explaining his innermost fantasy.

He was very concerned and afraid of being laughed at by his friends if he disclosed his thoughts. He just stood there while pretending to blend in with the conversations of his peers. It was a brutal time for Chad but he kept his composure.

Recess ended with a sigh and a groan by many. Chad knew there was only one more class to attend before lunch and that was too much for him. He had no choice but get through it the best he could.

That class lingered on but that did not stop him from the constant thought of the Painted Bunting. He, again, thought about telling his friends about his wondrous, morning confrontation but, somehow, with caution and his internal guide, refrained from doing so. He simply did not want to take that risk and regret it later. It was an agonizing conflict he had to endure.

Math class was quite demanding in thought and

computations. His concentration was thwarted in the least. He shunned away from as much as possible as he knew he would not be productive. The essence of working math was not present and he knew it very well. The clock on the wall was ticking slowly and discordantly.

Lunch period arrived but it is a mere thirty minutes and that included a quick recess before the next class began. Time seemed to take a vacation, Chad thought to himself. He sat with his friends but remained quiet and reserved in speaking. He did his best in not displaying his inner struggles with thoughts of the Painted Bunting.

The lunch period, as usual, ended quickly with a bell that gave all students a clear indication that the next class was at hand. The shuffle of feet and the constant sound of voices was so common throughout the hallway.

The afternoon schedule was impeccable in every way. Chad found himself doodling and not at all focused on classroom matters. The thought of his feathered friend was a powerful force within his mind. It consumed him intently with so much energy and control.

The three o'clock alarm sounded with much relief.

Chad left the classroom and quickly gathered his things at his locker. He exited the school building in a flash and did not think twice to say goodbye to any of his friends. It appeared that he was escaping a most horrific event.

"Wait up Chad! What's the hurry?" shouted John.

"Just anxious to get home. I have many chores to do before my father comes home," he said heedlessly. The excuse seemed to come naturally which was to his benefit.

"Chad, you are surely acting strange today. I hope it is nothing I've said or done," said John.

"No, not at all! I will call you later, okay?" Chad blurted as he hurried away.

He was not sure that was the right thing to say to John but he figured if he needed someone to talk to about his obsession, it would be John. He knew he would listen and possibly understand. It was a chance he needed to take and hoped for no regrets.

Chad arrived home and hurriedly entered without saying anything to his mom. He had high hopes and expectations of what could happen. His mother was somewhat concerned of his behavior but did not question him. She felt whatever was troubling him, he would eventually tell her. Time has a way of settling conflicts.

He walked slowly and quietly upstairs not to hinder a possible encounter with his feathered friend. Chad rested upon his neatly-made bed while gazing intently at the windowsill in hopes of greeting the Painted Bunting again. Chad attempted to create the most perfect image possible for his planned visit.

Suddenly, an enlivened and high-pitched chirp was heard as if it was only a hand-touch away. The afternoon breeze lifted the curtain to disclose his awaited friend. It was the Painted Bunting. It was perched on the windowsill with less fear and apprehension. The Painted Bunting seemed to know his arrival was welcomed and long-awaited.

Chad was motionless as he stared at this feathery beauty of red, green and blue colors. He wanted to pacify the encounter for as long as he could. He noted its keen sense of awareness of the surroundings as it looked around in all directions. Chad was tempted to approach the windowsill but self-control held the moment secure. He knew it was the right thing to do.

"How beautiful you are," Chad said softly. "How I wish I could fly and be free like you for even a short flight." The feeling was incredible and he wanted to say more. He was not sure of what to do next so he remained motionless.

The Painted Bunting appeared to comprehend what he said and that he had the power to grant that wish. Chad thought about that as well but knew that this would be incredulous. The communication between them was more than just a visual contact but seemed to have a feeling of mental telepathy that pacified the moment.

"Chad, your chores need to be done before your father arrives from work," his mother called out with a forceful voice.

She entered his room to find Chad lying on his bed and he suddenly displayed an obvious sigh of disappointment as his friend flew away from the assumed danger. The visitation ended abruptly and with much regret.

"Chad," she said impatiently. "Get up and do your chores like I told you!"

"Okay," he mumbled with sadness. He knew that it was imminent. He needed to get this done as his father would arrive home soon. Just maybe, he could have another chance of seeing the Painted Bunting before supper.

Chad quickly left his room and began his usual

chores. His father expected him to take care of the necessary things after school. He was a self-disciplined man who expected Chad to be the same. His father believed whole-heartedly that having personal expectations would promote self-worth and aspirations within one self. Chad knew, too well, what was expected of him and that he did not want to disappoint his parents.

His father was a physics professor at Rayton University just minutes from home. He was just like Mr. Freeman. He was intelligent and enjoyed teaching. He hoped that Chad would major in engineering at Rayton and be very successful in his career. He believed so much in Chad and knew that a constant reminder may help him remain focus to achieve his goals.

The chores were rather tedious at times but Chad knew it had to be done. His inner thoughts surrounded his every move while accomplishing every task. He worked methodically and efficiently. Time did take a toll and before he realized it, his father arrived and it was time for supper. He missed that opportunity to visit with the Painted Bunting.

Chad's mother called out loudly for him to come

in for supper. The chores that were not completed would have to wait until tomorrow.

"I'll be right there, mom," Chad said. As he walked toward the house, he could not help but glance upward toward his bedroom window that maybe, just maybe, he could see the Painted Bunting.

They all sat around the table as his father said the usual blessing before the meal. It was a family ritual to say the blessing. Great, family values were always top priority.

"How was your day at school?" asked his father.

"Very much the same," said Chad as he really did not feel like talking.

His mother was somewhat concerned of his response as she so often heard more of what he did at school. She saw the look of despair in Chad but did not want to make him uneasy in front of his father.

"Remember son, it is very important that you do well in school if you are to enter Rayton University after high school," said his dad.

"Yes sir" Chad responded.

Chad was very restless during the meal and hoped he would not give any indication to his parents that something was bothering him. The conversation at the dinner table was mostly between his mom and dad.

That was okay with him as his obsession occupied his thoughts totally.

When supper was over, they all helped in the kitchen and retreated to the den for some restful, quiet time. Chad mentioned that he would be in his room for some quiet reading. This was his excuse to escape and venture to his bedroom. He wished his parents goodnight and left the room hastily.

He entered his bedroom rather nervously but with much excitement. He approached his window and gazed into the night very cautiously. The clean-swept night breeze gave a sign of life outside. He wanted to be reassured that he had that chance of another encounter.

Chad had, undoubtedly, no more on his mind than the thought of the Painted Bunting. He calmly rested his limber body on the bed and created a mental dream of being totally free and uninhibited in flight. He closed his eyes to begin his secret journey into the limitless skies. He had longed for this moment all day and it finally arrived with many hours to experience his personal adventure.

The morning slowly arrived with a faintly-lit sky as the sun restored light for a new day. The time was six-thirty and all was extremely quiet. Chad's flight-filled dream ended abruptly as he felt a powerful feeling impact his body. The jamming jolt and the ferocious force awakened him in a consciousness so unfamiliar to him. He was surrounded by things and images so frightful and baffling. Chad realized that he was perched on a branch hanging gracefully from the tall, oak tree just outside his bedroom window.

Chad looked at himself and he was in bright array of colors of red, green and blue. Suddenly, a familiar voice was heard from the kitchen below. It was the voice of his mom calling out to him.

"Chad, wake up! Breakfast is ready."

Chad did not respond. His mother called out again with a more forceful voice, but this time Chad responded with a short, chirping sound.

Her concern prompted her to walk upstairs and open his bedroom door. Again, she called out his name and he chirped as loud as he could. She walked over to his window as the morning breeze lifted the curtain ever so slightly. She called out his name in a panic-stricken voice and still no answer. All she heard was a chirp.

Chad's mother noticed a beautiful bird perched on a branch nearby. She was fixated on its calming effect on her, but strangely, at the same time, she felt anxious. The silent communication between them was very powerful but misunderstood by his mother. She felt hopeless and was not able to grasp what was happening.

As the new Painted Bunting stood perched on the branch, he realized that he should be resting in bed experiencing the aroma of a home-cooked breakfast. He had to get ready for school, but he must turn and fly away. He knew that his dream became reality and that the old Chad would no longer be but a memory. He knew that his new life would be to explore a whole new world; a world of gliding and landing in the most interesting places.

He flew away with grateful feelings of freedom, chirping goodbye to his bedroom dreams. The flap of his wings was his way of saying goodbye to his mom. As she witnessed the flight of the Painted Bunting, she felt an unexplained loss within her. The feeling was unbearable to her as tears filled her eyes. She was speechless. Simply, there wasn't anything she could do.

Chad was a novice at flying, but he knew that time would give him expertise in turns and swirls. He knew that the sky is now his home. The time arrived for his new-found adventure in the limitless skies. It was what he wished for and it was granted.

As he glided toward a cluster of oak trees, he felt impelled to explore. Next to the trees was a two-story house. The upstairs window was very inviting as the limbs of the towering trees hung gracefully near it and gave it shade to the windowsill below.

Chad landed cautiously as the wind-swept breeze lifted the curtains just enough to display a bedroom occupied by a young girl. He recognized her as one of his classmates named Sherri. She was just awakened by his early morning visit. She gazed at him intently and studied his every move. Chad seemed to comprehend her wish. He felt impelled to grant her wish. He was quite familiar with that feeling as it clearly happened to him. They both looked at each other as though it was the most powerful experience one could have.

"How I wish I could fly and be free like you for even a short flight," she said quietly to herself.

AMARYLLIS

A long-awaited summer by two, young, adventurous boys was noted by a mysterious and unexplainable phenomenon, one of which became an everlasting experience. It created an eccentric journey to a world so attracted to them and it became a matter of having a second chance.

Phil and Matt attended Serenity Springs Junior High located in Serenity Springs. The town was nestled between two mountain ranges which gave this locale the most unique place to live. It was small, quaint and historic with few activities to offer but that did not stop Phil and Matt from creating some adventure of their own. Time was on their side for a change as it was summer break from school.

They were not related but, somehow, through all the time spent together, they felt inseparable. Many townspeople referred to them as brothers and, the truth of the matter, they wished they were. Living in the same neighborhood, they accompanied each other in all they did.

This day seemed like any other day; however, something prompted them to do something different. It was mid-morning and it was a great day to be outdoors. They always considered themselves unique outdoorsmen in Serenity Springs.

"Do you want to go hiking up in the foothills today?" asked Phil.

"Sure! Let's go."

It was only a matter of minutes that they got their gear together. Phil was meticulous and methodical in preparation to go hiking or anything else for that matter. It seemed that he had a mental checklist of all sorts of things that he would need. He took surviving to the next level. They informed their moms and off they went like soldiers on a mission.

It was nine thirty-four in the morning as Matt

checked his waterproof watch with precision. Their usual path for hiking was familiar to them as they have hiked it many times before. Today; however, they hoped for something new and challenging. They did not want this day to be monotonous.

It did not take long when Phil and Matt decided to change their usual course. The new trail taken was unspoiled. With backpacks on their back and canteens at their side, the forthcoming adventure was at hand.

They were novices on this trail and so they looked at everything with amazement. Their usual conversation was hampered at times because of the interesting environment around them. It kept their attention at every turn. The path taken soon led them to a narrow clearing which marked the end of the trail.

They stopped for a quick drink and a short rest. They looked around and felt bold and daring to create their own path through thick weeds and brush. They felt camouflaged from the world they knew. They did not think about retreating from the unknown.

Phil reached into his pocket and pulled out his compass. "We are heading northwest at this time," he said with certainty.

He assumed the position as leader and felt the

need to keep their direction in check. He took his leadership seriously and without reluctance.

Clearing their own path slowed their forward progress but it was all worth it. Pulling branches and twigs to one side for each other was tedious but rewarding. They knew that teamwork was something they always had in common with each other.

It was hot and humid but the constant struggle of creating their own path was captivating. They stopped occasionally to get a quick sip of water and a rest.

"Do you think we will remember our way back?" asked Matt with some concern.

"I suppose so," said Phil. "Maybe we should use markers to help us."

He reached into his backpack and pulled out a roll of red ribbon. Phil had the knack of having a supply of survival items.

"This will work just fine if we tie short pieces around the tree branches along the trail."

They cut small strips of ribbon just long enough to tie around each small branch. They did this sparingly as they were not sure how far they would hike. They staged their steps carefully and methodically along the way as they fastened a ribbon around a branch or twig. This was done every fifty feet or so.

Phil checked his compass several times along the way. It gave him confidence as a leader to keep abreast of their journey. Phil's intuition kept them progressing in the direction taken.

They reached another clearing with relief as they needed a rest and another drink. The heat was stifling as they sweated profusely. The surrounding trees kept any breeze from filtering through to them. Even with these conditions, the seclusion was still mysterious to say the least.

"What do we do now?" asked Matt.

"Well, let me check my watch."

To their surprise, the time was twelve-thirty. They were amazed how much time passed while clearing the trail.

After several short gulps of water from their canteens, they were ready to proceed. They merged their resources together as Phil led the way.

With astonishment, they both focused on a nearby, partially hidden cave between two, giant boulders. The opening to the cave was enchanting. It intercepted their forward progress with a mesmerizing effect.

The newly-found cave had a narrow passage partially hidden by thick shrubbery. The entrance was just wide enough for one person to walk in at one time.

It was a minimal risk and they concerted to enter. Phil entered first with his flashlight secured tightly in his hand. Matt immediately followed him with some apprehension.

"Wow!" said Phil. "This is an awesome cave," he said with amazement.

Phil focused his flashlight toward mysterious markings and carvings on the wall.

"The markings look ancient," said Matt.

It appeared there were names and initials of people who traveled this path before. Some names had dates showing years past. It was as though you needed to sign your permission into the cave.

Phil and Matt wanted to add their names to the list as well. They each picked up a small rock nearby and engraved their identity with precision. It gave them a small ownership to the cave.

"Okay. We need to get going!" Phil said.

They proceeded with limited light along the meandering path. It was very interesting at every turn with stalactites and stalagmites around them. The scenery was something they did not ever see before and it was almost indescribable.

Phil looked at his compass and it showed they

were headed due north. That did not mean anything as the trail continuously changed in many directions.

The path had several merging trails that created uncertainty at every turn. Their quest was doubtful but they kept moving forward. They seemed to have an intuition of traveling in the right direction. Phil's flashlight was their only beacon to somewhere.

Suddenly, they both heard a remote sound coming from around the bend. It was an unfamiliar sound as it created an echo off the cave walls. They both paused to listen intently to determine what it was. They continued to track tirelessly toward the unknown.

The sound guided them through every turn on the trail. It eventually muted any communication between them. Their journey was so uncertain and mystifying.

They continued their path in the direction they assumed was correct. It became louder with every step taken. They came this far and now it was unavoidable to seek the source up ahead. They could not turn back.

Suddenly to their amazement, the mystery was solved.

"It is a waterfall!" Matt said with excitement.

They rushed toward it but with extreme caution. They were in awe to see the fast-moving stream that flowed ferociously out of the cave into a large pool below.

They both sat down on a huge, crystalline rock just steps away from the stream. The waterfall's crashing turbulence hypnotized them. The sound was almost unbearable. It resonated off the walls of the cave with power and consistency. The current of the water was rapid and powerful yet it gave a sense of protection.

As they sat there, Phil decided to check his compass once more. As he focused his eyes upon the compass needle, it was spinning haphazardly without any distinct direction.

"What is going on?" Phil said with disbelief.

Matt also looked at the compass and said "What do we do now?"

At that moment, Matt felt his watch vibrating violently. The needle of time was twirling out of control.

"Look, my watch is doing the same thing!"

They both stood with fear and indecisiveness as what to do next.

Simultaneously, they turned away from the waterfall to retreat away from uncertainty. A stumble and a strange, intense push projected their bodies into the stream and down the waterfall. Phil and Matt yelled as they plummeted into the large pool below. The turbulence of the water twisted and distorted every move attempted by Phil and Matt. It kept them submerged as they fought with intensity.

They surfaced into a thick cloud of mist that surrounded them. They swam helplessly to the pool's edge as it held them captive the entire time. Tired and soaked, they managed to crawl out to safety. They were resilient through the horrific ordeal.

Phil and Matt sat in amazement, as they witnessed the new-found land. It was one they had never seen before. They were speechless. The beauty it possessed was unbelievable. The mist from the waterfall gave their surroundings an eerie feeling yet one of security.

"Where are we?" said Matt.

"I don't know!" Phil said in a shivering voice.

Out in a distant, two young people walked toward them. It was a welcomed sight for Phil and Matt since they did not know where they were.

"Maybe, they can help us," said Matt.

They immediately showed concern about their well-being. "Are you okay?" asked the young boy.

"Yes we are!" responded Phil.

"I am Tom and this is Susan. Who are you?" Tom asked.

"I am Phil and this is my best friend Matt. Where are we?"

"You are in Amaryllis, the hidden valley of the world above. You have arrived here on Hidden Falls, the only way into this land. We truly welcome you here," Tom said graciously.

"We are glad you are here to join us," said Susan.

Phil was skeptical of what he heard and wanted to know more. "I do not understand what has happened to us!"

"This land was found by several of us many years ago when we hiked into Secrecy Cave. We decided to stay and make this our permanent home," Tom said.

"Several years ago?" asked Phil, with total confusion.

"Yes! We live here and we do not age," said Susan. "It is one of the benefits of living here in Amaryllis. We have accepted our new world. Everything here is perfect for us. Initially, we were homesick but we have made this land our own."

"Did you notice the initials and names on the cave wall as you entered Secrecy Cave? It is our signage of acceptance," said Tom.

"Yes, we did. In fact, we signed our name on the wall as well," said Matt.

"But where did this world come from?" Matt asked.

"I'll come to that later," Tom responded patiently.

"Let me show you around Amaryllis first and then we can talk more, later. We have a lot to discuss with you and Phil."

He gave them a brief tour of the land. It was so peaceful and inviting as the beauty lured them to seek more. Everything about Amaryllis was perfect as mentioned before by Tom. Beautiful flowers and trees outlined the landscape around them. Phil and Matt were held in suspense. Every moment in time seemed to stand still with no explanation.

"Where are the rest of the people here?" asked Matt.

"Well, you will meet them later if you decide to stay with us," said Tom.

Matt looked at his watch. To his surprise, it was four-thirty and they needed to leave immediately. He was concerned that his mom would be upset if they got back home late.

"Phil, let's leave now!" Matt said forcefully. "We can come back tomorrow!"

They left frantically and headed toward the

waterfall. They neglected to say goodbye as they left so quickly.

Phil and Matt ran up the side of the waterfall and climbed vigorously to the top.

"Wait! Wait! Wait!" Tom repeatedly yelled. The loud, turbulent sound of the crashing waterfall hindered them from hearing Tom's plea.

Upon reaching the top and with shortness of breath, they both just waved to Tom and Susan down below. Tom again, repeated for them to wait but to no avail. It was too late. Phil and Matt turned abruptly and headed back down the winding path.

Phil's compass and Matt's watch spiraled out of control again as it did before. They did not care at that moment. Getting home was their only concern. Phil sensed they were leaving one world and entering another.

They ran down the path hastily as Phil led the way with his flashlight held tightly. They were agile at every turn along the path. There wasn't an obstacle that could slow them down.

They noticed a small ray of light coming from the outside world as they approached the entrance to Secrecy Cave. It was a welcomed relief from the trail just traveled. It guided their departure and gave them fortitude to escape the unknown.

They squeezed through the small opening quickly. Within seconds, they headed down the marked path back home. Without any words spoken, they ran as fast as they glimpsed at the ribbons along the way. They did not stop to rest or drink any water.

Phil and Matt ran faster than they ever thought they could. The thick brush and hanging branches scraped their bodies every step of the way. They showed solidarity in their journey back.

When they arrived home, they both fell to the ground with exhaustion. Phil's mom rushed outside and asked where were they.

"I have been worried about you both!" she said frantically.

"We were out exploring this neat cave, Mom," said Phil.

"Well, you both get ready for supper. Matt can stay for the evening if he calls his mom."

That was perfect for them. They had so much to talk about. What happened was too mysterious to forget and too adventurous not to return.

"We have to go back tomorrow," said Matt.

"For sure, we have to!" Phil responded.

That evening, they were consumed with the journey they experienced. They planned an early hike the next morning so Matt set the alarm on his watch. They even struggled to fall asleep. They relived every moment as though it was still happening. Eventually, they fell asleep from exhaustion.

Phil and Matt awoke before the alarm sounded. They were too anxious to return to their cave. It even haunted them during their sleep. It consumed them and would not let go.

After a quick breakfast, they gathered their gear with a fresh supply of water for their canteens. They told Phil's mom goodbye and headed out the door.

"I want you both to be very careful. I expect you back by four o'clock this afternoon, Phil. We are going out of town to visit your grandmother," she said.

"Okay mom!" Phil responded.

Matt checked his watch and it was seven-thirty. This was so unusual that they were out and about at that time of the morning.

They hurriedly walked down their newly-discovered path again and entered the clearing as they did the day before. They had a mission to accomplish, so they did not waste any time.

Phil and Matt did not say a word. The only sounds

they heard was the huffing and puffing of quick, short breaths. The ribbons guided their way precisely back to Secrecy Cave.

Phil turned on his flashlight and proceeded incessantly into the cave. Matt followed closely behind. Phil could hear every footstep behind him. They stomped courageously along the meandering path to the waterfall. The compass and the watch spun out of control again, but that did not alarm them.

Again, the roaring sound of the waterfall kept them from communicating. Using a hand signal, Phil pointed for them to stand close to the edge of the stream. Matt agreed with eagerness as he trusted his best friend.

Phil and Matt simultaneously stepped onto the slippery rock right at the edge as planned which propelled their bodies into the pool below. This time they yelled with excitement as they plunged into the cool waters. They did not feel the unexplained force which held them before. It was a more simplistic venture this time.

They swam to the pool's edge and climbed out. Tom was waiting for them as he knew they would come back to Amaryllis.

"Hi Tom!" said Phil.

"Hi! I knew that you would be back soon. The temptation of this beautiful land is far too great to ignore," replied Tom.

"I am sorry that you left so suddenly yesterday. You did not wait to hear what I had to tell you on your quick departure."

"We are sorry too but we had to get home soon," said Matt.

"Come with me. Let me show you more of Amaryllis. You will also get to meet the rest of us who live here," said Tom. "They are anxious to visit with you and Matt."

"As I said before, the animals here are friendly. The majestic trees, beautiful flowers, crisp air and clear, blue skies made us stay. Amaryllis provides everything we want and need," said Tom.

"Why is this land called Amaryllis?" asked Phil.

"The name Amaryllis was decided years ago because of the abundance of the many kinds of Amaryllis flowers throughout the land," said Tom.

The final tour of the land was one that Phil and Matt would never forget. This land was so vast and appeared to go on forever. It was totally tantalizing to Phil and Matt as they looked with awe at everything Tom showed them. The scenery was overwhelming and breath-taking. The tour took several hours and without one disappointment.

"When will we meet the rest of your friends?" asked Phil.

"They will visit with you soon," said Tom. "They are preparing for your stay here."

Matt looked at his watch and he knew it was time again for them to leave.

"We will see you tomorrow. We can spend time visiting your friends when we return," said Phil.

Tom said "Wait! I need to inform you of something very important. It is something you failed to hear as you left so quickly yesterday."

"What is that?" Phil asked with much concern.

Tom carefully spoke to Phil and Matt so they would understand. "You have only two chances to enter Amaryllis. After that, this land becomes your permanent home."

"I do not understand what you are saying," Matt responded fearfully. Tom spoke calmly as not to scare them into another attempted, quick getaway.

"Just listen to me carefully as I explain to you what has happened," said Tom. "This land is the hidden land of enchantment. It is unseen by many and held only by a few. It gives you a chance to enter and re-enter if you wish. It gives you a chance to experience the beauty and serenity. If you choose to come back the second time, this home is yours to keep with no return back to the other world. The point of no return is Hidden Falls."

"This is nonsense Tom!" said Matt with anger and disbelief. They heard enough of this nonsense.

Without saying goodbye, they quickly turned and ran toward the rock wall near the edge of Hidden Falls. They climbed furiously and with determination to reach the top. As they approached the summit of Hidden Falls, an unexplained force pulled them back into the pool below. They immediately climbed out of the pool and attempted once more. They were defeated again. They failed again and again, no matter what they attempted.

The rest of Tom's friends assembled at the edge of the pool in support of their unsuccessful feat. They all looked at Phil and Matt with helpless intentions. They could not aid them in any way.

Phil and Matt were drained of energy in their flight to return home. Their resistance to stay was overcome by Amaryllis. Their attempt to escape was intercepted by destiny.

What turned out to be the most powerful force in

Amaryllis was not the beauty but the inescapable ties to the land. All of the beauty it possessed was much less than the old world they knew. They were held captive in a world, regardless of their desire. Amaryllis kept them harnessed from ever returning back to Serenity Springs.

Phil and Matt knew they were defeated. They no longer had the choice to leave, no matter what they did. Their quest into Amaryllis was their fate all along and did not know it.

"Goodbye Mom," Phil said.

"Yes, goodbye Mom," Matt said also.

With sadness shown in their faces and the disappointment of defeat, they knew that their second chance was taken. They simply had to accept the outcome.

They could never be home in time for supper. They could never be home in time, ever!

TRIPPER

This mysterious occurrence began with much concern as it shared some very powerful feelings of a long, lost friend from the past. Stuart, an eight year old, was just a happy, normal boy who confronted the usual gift of make-believe and curiosity. His thoughts of friendship and loneliness were on his mind quite often possibly because he was an only child in the family. He was a creative young boy and suggestive ideas kept him occupied during the day.

Breakfast was served at the usual time every morning at six-thirty on school days. His mother was very adamant about having a good meal to begin the day. Stuart was seated at the kitchen table as the aroma of eggs and bacon filled the room.

His dad entered the kitchen and said, "Good morning everyone!" in a very cheerful manner.

Mr. Carter was extremely excited since he anticipated a promotion after twelve successful years as an office supervisor for Turner Industries. His dedication to his profession was ready to pay off and be promoted to an executive position of the company. Needless to say, his thoughts were mainly on the interview and the final decision. Nothing else seemed to matter at the moment.

Joey's dad was very talkative at breakfast and his mom gave her undivided attention. She knew that this position was something he worked hard to achieve. Stuart awaited his turn in conversation and he finally had the chance.

"Dad, why did you leave Tripper?"

"Who is Tripper?" asked his dad.

"My friend!" Stuart responded quickly.

His father, with much on his mind, ignored Stuart and quickly drank the remaining coffee in his cup. His brief encounter at breakfast heeded to his immediate exit out the door.

"I will see you both later. Have a great day at school, Stuart," he said in a cheerful voice.

"I wish you the best," Joey's mom responded.

Stuart was disappointed that his dad did not have more to say about his friend. His mom did not inquire either as she was busy cleaning up the kitchen after breakfast. Stuart just accepted it for the moment and knew that he would have another opportunity to talk to his dad when he returned from work.

Mrs. Carter was very prompt on her daily routine. She took care of Stuart as any good mother would. Stuart knew all too well that his mom was a great mom and he was fortunate to have her.

"It is time to leave, Stuart. You don't want to be late for school," she said.

"Okay Mom."

He quickly grabbed his lunch bag and backpack from the kitchen with a solemn look on his face.

"Is everything okay?" his mom asked.

"Sure," Stuart said.

The trip to school was rather uneventful especially in conversation. She noticed that he was extremely quiet and preoccupied.

"What's on your mind?" she asked.

Stuart, simply, shrugged his shoulders indicating

that nothing was wrong. He was deep in thought during the fifteen minute trip to Longville Elementary School.

Stuart had a lot on his mind. His make-believe friend was hurt and bewildered over his dad's response at the kitchen table this morning. Stuart, too, was confused and hurt. He expected a more compassionate response and wished his dad would have taken his concern more seriously.

They arrived at school with only five minutes to spare. Stuart gave his mom a quick kiss and a goodbye gesture. He did not fail to acknowledge his friend, Tripper.

"Bye Tripper. See you later!"

His mom was puzzled by what he said but made no comment.

"Have a great day at school, Stuart. See you this afternoon," she said.

Stuart hurriedly laid his backpack down and ran toward his group of friends. They always played near the front entrance of the building. Soon, the bell rang and they all lined up as his teacher instructed them to enter the hallway quietly.

The day seemed longer than usual since Stuart had Tripper on his mind. He thought about him all day long. Stuart knew that it was imperative to find out why his father did not know who was Tripper.

When Stuart's mom picked him up after school, she noticed that he was quiet yet anxious.

"How was your day at school?" asked his mom.

"Oh, it was okay, I guess." Stuart responded.

Stuart looked around and did not see Tripper.

"Where is Tripper?" Stuart asked.

"Who is Tripper?" She responded.

Stuart did not answer. He was too upset and did not want to say anymore. The solitude Stuart displayed was of deep concern by his mom.

When Stuart arrived at home, he ran to his room to confront Tripper. He knew that Tripper would be there. He saw him sitting in his chair with a sad look on his face.

"How was your day today, Tripper?" asked Stuart as he embraced him with sincerity. "I was worried about you when you were not in the car."

Stuart was very concerned about his friend's feelings and just wanted everything to be okay. Time would only tell. Stuart felt that Tripper was his only loyal companion. Tripper was an ideal friend that was trustworthy and kind, no matter what happened.

"But why did my father leave you?" asked Stuart as he looked at Tripper.

The feelings were mutual and Stuart knew that time was near to ask his father again. He could only hope for an answer that would suffice his curiosity.

Stuart was very eager to go to his clubhouse so he changed into his play clothes and hurriedly left his room. As usual, Tripper was there behind his every footstep but with a bleak look on his face. They both walk with a sense of fortitude and wanted to pacify each other.

"Mom, I will be in my clubhouse," Stuart said.

"Okay. Your dad will be home soon and maybe he will have great news to tell us."

The clubhouse was a place of retreat and ownership among the two. It was located in the backyard about fifty yards away from the house and secluded among many large trees. It was sturdily built and secured about ten feet above ground in the arm of an old, colossal oak tree. This was a location selected by his father years ago when he was a young child. The years of weathering and use played a stern toll it; however, that made it more attractive to them.

Stuart's clubhouse portrayed a robust look to it. It was a place where Stuart and Tripper spent most of their free time to talk and play. It became the fortress from the rest of the world. It was their private sanctum.

Mrs. Carter glanced many times in the backyard to see if Stuart was okay. She was worried about his strange behavior.

Stuart and Tripper played for a couple of hours. They always had a great time in the clubhouse.

"Stuart, it is time for supper,"

Stuart responded, "Okay! We'll be there in a second!" He knew it was the moment he was waiting for but he felt extremely anxious.

"Well, we have to go now, Tripper. I will ask my father again. You can count on me," he said with assurance.

Tripper just followed him side by side like intrepid companions ought to be. Stuart felt a sense of relief as he knew Tripper would be next to him as support.

Stuart entered the kitchen and saw his dad and mom seated at the kitchen table. He quickly washed his hands and sat nervously with Tripper by his side. Stuart wanted the time to be right when he would ask his father again.

Mr. Carter was very cheerful and at that moment Stuart knew that his father received the promotion. Again, the total conversation was about his job and felt he had no chance to ask his father. He was simply a spectator and did not want to spoil the excitement.

"How was your day at school Stuart?" asked his dad.

"Okay," he said.

"That's all you have to say?" his dad responded.

Stuart did not say anything. He was deep in thought as what to say to his father later.

When supper was over, he sought to find the most opportune moment to speak to him. It came shortly after his father retreated to his favorite chair in the den. Stuart hoped that his father would listen without any interruptions.

"Dad" remarked Stuart, "Why did you leave Tripper?"

"Who is Tripper?" asked his father as he showed more interest.

"He is my friend!" said Stuart.

With deep curiosity, "When did I leave him?" asked his father.

"You left him many years ago when you were my age," he said with sadness and despair. "You hurt him and he is confused. He felt that you abandoned him without any reason!"

At that moment, his father seemed confused as

well. "I am not sure I understand what you are telling me." He was perplexed at what he heard.

Stuart was so nervous but needed to do this for Tripper. He took a deep breath and held his composure.

"Dad, did you ever have a friend that was there for you and always played with you in your clubhouse when you were a child?" Stuart said with a dismal look on his face.

"Sure I did but what does that have to do with me and your friend?" his dad responded.

"Well Dad, Tripper was your friend also."

A moment of silence followed as Mr. Carter tried to put all he heard in perspective. He desperately tried to make sense of all of this.

"How do you know I had a friend named Tripper?"

"Because he told me so," said Stuart.

"What?"

"Yes Dad! He told me!"

Suddenly, it became quite evident that he remembered part of his past. He was speechless. He gazed at Stuart with a horrified look. He never told anyone of his make-believe friend he had as a child.

Stuart's mom entered the room slowly and with

a questionable look on her face asked, "Dear, what is going on?"

Stuart's dad did not respond as he was shocked in disbelief of the knowledge he had gained.

With a lurid stare in his eyes, he asked, "Where is Tripper today?"

With eagerness to answer, "He is right here sitting next to me with tears in his eyes."

"What? Is he right here in this room?" asked Mr. Carter.

"Yes."

"Can he hear me?" asked his father.

"Sure he can. Tripper just wants to know why you left him years ago," said Stuart. "He feels hurt that you don't remember him after all the time you both spent together as friends."

Mrs. Carter stood there in a total state of shock. She did not understand any part of the conversation.

Stuart's dad just sat there without anything to say. He was lost and confused about the whole situation.

Finally, after a short period of silence, he asked, "How long have you known that I had a make-believe friend named Tripper?"

"He told me a couple of weeks ago, Dad. He told me a lot about how much you both shared together as friends. He remembered all the fun and the time spent in the clubhouse."

Mr. Carter was convinced that Stuart was involved with something very powerful and he could not explain it. It was so surreal.

At that moment, Tripper, Stuart and his dad left the room and ruefully walked toward the clubhouse. Stuart's dad knew that so many things needed to be unveiled.

They walked in unison without conversing as though they needed time to ponder on the reality of the moment. It was a time of silence to reminisce until they arrived on common ground again. It was a moment of truth and affirmation of a time well-spent.

As they climbed up the tree to the clubhouse, a sense of renewal and youth overcame Mr. Carter. He attained his secret journey back in time to be with his long-forgotten friend, Tripper.

He turned toward Stuart and said "I am very sorry to you and Tripper. I do not want this to happen again!"

Tears of joy filled their faces. Stuart and Tripper felt a sense of relief from the nervousness and anxiety they had for some time.

"It is okay, Dad. He is happy now. He is so excited

that you remembered him and that you still care about him," said Stuart.

"Can I hug you both?" asked his Dad.

"Yes, you can," Stuart said without hesitation.

He, courageously, hugged Stuart and Tripper. He, again, admitted he was sorry. The visions of his early childhood raced across his mind. His faith in his youth was revived again. His once callous lack of memory of his past quickly vanished and a new beginning had arrived.

They sat there and gazed at the sturdily-built clubhouse and talked about what they shared as friends. The laughter rang across the backyard as they played in the clubhouse without interruption.

Since the reunion of Tripper, they spent time everyday together at their secluded retreat. It became a daily ritual of fun.

Stuart's mom still does not know the details of what transpired that day. She knows for certain that it created endless hours for Stuart and his dad to reminisce about the good times he had when he was a child, especially with Tripper.

They are so fortunate to have this special comradery. It took an indelible memory in his life to recapture the past.

Many years have elapsed and it demanded Stuart to share his past with his own son. Stuart remembered to tell him about Tripper. It was a great time well-spent with each other in the same weathered clubhouse located on the arm of an old, colossal oak tree in the same backyard. It became a common ground of memories for eternity.

THE RELIC

A June summer day in 2015 was a usual hot and humid one in Oak Town, Louisiana. It was a cozy and quaint town. Huge oak and cypress trees streamed along main street and outlying areas which made it a picturesque place to live. Anyone who was a resident in Oak Town could tell you that it was quite satisfying in so many ways, especially, its close proximity to great fishing and hunting areas.

It was a typical day, one might imagine, except for two young boys searching for an escape from boredom. It was summer break and they beckoned for relief. Joey and Steve were best friends who had many things in common, one of which was fishing. When the opportunity arose, fishing took precedence over most other things.

It was late Tuesday morning and fishing at nearby Cypress Pond came to mind. Their assigned chores were completed and had plenty of time on their hands.

Cypress Pond was a huge pond only a mile from town, about an hour's walk up an unpaved road. That location provided the opportunity to catch many catfish and bream. It did not matter what fish was swimming in the pond, but the challenge of the catch and the hope of a fish fry.

Joey quickly suggested that they go to Cypress Pond and try their luck at fishing. They fished there several times before and it was considered one of the best places.

"Yes, as soon as I can get my pole and tackle box," said Steve.

"Awesome!" responded Joey.

Steve lived just a few houses down from Joey which made it quite convenient, especially when plans were done at the spur of the moment. He left quickly to get what he needed to fish and returned to meet Joey.

Joey seemed in charge most of the time while Steve followed along with the plans. Nevertheless, they got along very well and seem to compliment their differences. Steve, on the other hand, was more methodical in his thoughts and actions. The solidarity of their friendship was their greatest asset.

They soon had their poles and tackle boxes in hand with optimism on their side. They knew that a fish fry this evening was inevitable.

"Let's get going!" Joey said.

It was just a brief walk from his house before he came up with another idea.

"Let's take a short cut to Cypress Pond," suggested Joey.

"Okay, Let's do it."

Joey made a quick left in a nearby field owned by Mr. Coulter, a retired farmer. They knew he would not mind since the property was not used for farming anymore. Joey and Steve headed west to merge onto Oak Alley Road.

The detour proved to be a challenging one as this

path was never taken before. The crackling sound of their footsteps upon tall grass, twigs and leaves made this walk a little more interesting. They looked at these obstacles as a test of character.

"I can see the road up ahead," Joey said with some relief in his voice.

"Great!" Steve said. "It's about time!"

They finally reached Oak Alley Road with much anticipation. They both turned and glanced back at the path taken as it seemed captivating and mysterious. The brisk breeze rustled the tall weeds nearby as it seemed to tell them something. Maybe, it was a subtle sign of what's to come.

Oak Alley Road is located on the outskirts of town and it is seldom used. Many years ago; however, it was a road that was traveled frequently. It is now overgrown with shrubs and brush that outline the edge of the road.

"Alright Steve, we will soon be there," Joey said excitingly.

"I think we will have many fish to catch. I can't wait!" The anticipation was almost as great as the fishing itself.

Their journey was hasty and without incidence.

The road less traveled gave them independence and courage.

They approached Cypress Pond and noticed that the water sparkled brilliantly in the sunlight. It was so quiet you could almost hear your heart beating. The pond was surrounded by large Cypress trees and seemed to have power to protect its existence from any unwanted guests.

They quickly claimed their personal spot located right at the water's edge. It was quite a unique fishing spot with much shade and a comfortable place to sit. It was the solitude they needed for fishing.

"Wow!" said Steve. "This seems to be the most perfect spot yet!"

The shade from a huge cypress tree and a gentle breeze provided relief from the heat.

They both agreed that this was the place. The chosen spot seemed unspoiled in every way. Although, it appeared that way, evidence of a past visitor was visible. An old soft drink bottle was seen nestled among weeds near the base of a nearby tree.

Joey and Steve were very versatile in all they did together. Steve managed to keep things organized and simplistic. Joey took things in stride and did not allow for uncertainties to bother him. Nonetheless, they got their gear in position for an exciting time at fishing. Everything went as planned.

They were not novices at this, so they did not waste any time to put their bait on their hooks and gently lowered their poles into the pond. Joey sat near the base of the tree while Steve chose a more rugged spot with a closer locale to the water's edge. Speaking was at a minimal as they patiently watched and waited for the sign of life to appear just beneath the surface of the water.

The peacefulness of their surroundings was a treat in itself as they intently gazed across the pond and waited for the first catch of the day. The water was so calm, it appeared like glass. Not a sound was heard except for a tweet from a small Finch on a nearby branch. The seclusion of Cypress Pond created a perfect environment to fish. It seemed that time wanted to stop, just for them.

Joey could not refrain from looking around between his short glimpses at the water. It was his character to view other things around him. It did not take much for him to divert his attention elsewhere. Steve, on the other hand, stared at the water as though he could send telepathic messages to the fish below.

Joey, in his wondering state of mind, noticed a

round, circular object just inches away from where he was sitting. He gently laid his pole down on the ground not to hinder any potential bite. He gently picked up the new-found relic. Without saying a word at first, he looked at it with much curiosity.

"I caught something," Steve uttered in a quiet tone. "I think I caught a catfish!"

"Great Steve!" responded Joey.

He wished he had the first catch of the day but that was okay. He knew that anything caught was considered caught by both of them.

"Hey Steve, come over here and take a look at this!" Joey whispered.

Steve leaned his pole against the tree trunk and quietly walked over to Joey. Joey continued to rub the residue off of the relic to determine exactly what it was. To his surprise, it was a coin.

Their interest quickly changed from fishing to fascination. Joey, vigorously, rubbed the relic until he was able to determine exactly what kind of coin it was.

"Wow!" he said with excitement. "It's a 1954 nickel!"

"Let me see it, Joey!" Steve said.

The nickel must have been on the ground for some time. It was extremely tarnished from the elements.

It had a dull look to it from all of the dirt and grime; however, it displayed a unique appearance.

"Hey, I wonder how much it's worth and who dropped it here Joey?" Steve asked. He always had a unique sense of curiosity about things.

"I don't know but I am glad I found it," responded Joey. He had a premonition that this coin was not just a regular coin but one of intricate value.

He placed the coin into his pocket and got back to fishing. Soon, Joey had his first catch as well. This gave him confidence that he, too, was successful.

"Congratulations Joey!" Steve said.

A couple more hours of fishing gave way to a dozen fish caught. It was more than they could imagine. This fishing trip proved to be more successful than the previous one. It was time to head back home.

They both became very talkative with no worry of scaring any fish away. Their mindset was getting home. The fish fry was just a mere forty-five minutes away.

"Joey, I can't wait to show mom and dad all the fish we caught!" said Steve.

"Yes! Me too!" said Joey as he held all the fish on the stringer.

Even though they were excited to get back home,

they took a leisurely walk down Oak Alley Road. They didn't feel the need to rush home. Time was on their side.

They soon stopped half-way up the road for a quick break. A tall oak tree provided a shady spot for them to sit and rest awhile on a nearby log. It was a welcomed retreat from the heat.

"Things could not get any better than this," exclaimed Steve.

Steve remembered the old coin Joey found and asked if he could see it again.

"Sure," responded Joey.

He sorted through the coins he had in his pocket. It was apparent which one was the 1954 coin since it had a dull look to it. Time does take a toll on things of old.

"I wonder who dropped it?" Steve asked again.

"I do not know. It's very interesting that it is a 1954 nickel," responded Joey.

"Maybe, the coin belonged to someone years ago who fished in that same spot," Steve said.

"Perhaps," he responded.

"Do you ever wonder how Oak Town looked back then and if many people fished at Cypress Pond?" asked Steve with continued curiosity.

"Yes I have. My dad has been in this town for thirty years and he told me a few interesting stories. Well, I know for sure, it's time for us to get going!" as Joey placed the coins back into his pocket.

They picked up their gear and the fish they so proudly caught. They walked side by side down the dirt road without a care in the world. They were fearless fishermen of Cypress Pond.

Joey and Steve suddenly stopped in their tracks as they encountered a vision that completely startled them. Approximately twenty yards ahead was a sight so bewildering to them. It was definitely something beyond their imagination.

It was a building nestled between two large oak trees. A bright, colorful sign hung on the front of the building that read TATE'S GROCERY. Directly in front was an old-time gas pump from the past. The price for gas was twenty-one cents.

"Look! It's a grocery store," Steve said. Joey did not respond.

It was a strange sight, but what was most bizarre was that the sign on the front read OPEN FOR BUSINESS.

"Where did that store come from?" asked Steve.

"I don't know," said Joey in disbelief. "It wasn't here this morning!"

Joey and Steve approached the front of the store slowly and cautiously. They were not sure of what to expect.

Joey gazed at the grocery signs displayed on the wall as unusual billboards of times past. They stepped onto the front porch with apprehension and disbelief. The old cypress boards creaked with every short step taken.

Suddenly, a man opened the screen door and walked onto the porch. He was the store keeper of the grocery store. They were surprised to see someone there.

"Can I help you boys?" he asked.

Totally confused and practically lost for words Joey responded "Uh, we are just….just……uh looking around."

"Come on in! You both look very thirsty!" he said with authority.

Joey and Steve simply followed his command and entered the grocery store. Immediately they realized that it was a blast from the past.

"My name is Mr. Tate. I am the owner of this store," he said with a chuckle.

"My name is Joey and this is my best friend, Steve. We were fishing today at Cypress Pond."

"Oh yeah, that famous fishing pond! I went fishing there yesterday. Did you catch any fish?"

"Yeah, a few," Joey said proudly.

"You both need each a milkshake to celebrate. What flavor? Chocolate or vanilla?"

They both responded, "Chocolate."

"You boys sit at the counter while I get your milkshakes. Make yourself at home," he said with a friendly smile.

Joey and Steve were lured to the counter with an unexplainable force. They sat on swivel stools of old, watching every move made by Mr. Tate.

He quickly got right to work to prepare their milkshakes as Joey and Steve stared in disbelief. The fact that they were the only ones in the store was also quite mysterious.

The strangeness of everything around them warranted the idea that this was, indeed, not of the present. The entire store was outdated in the least. Joey and Steve were held captive in a time not familiar to them.

"Where did this store come from?" asked Joey.

"What do you mean?" questioned Mr. Tate with a puzzled look on his face.

"We walked this way this morning and didn't see this store. We never saw this here before," said Joey. Steve was silent during the whole conversation. He was still in awe as he curiously scanned every direction within the store.

"This store has been here for some time. Where have you been? I bought it ten years ago! Do you live in Oak Town?" Mr. Tate kindly asked.

"Yes, we do!" Joey quickly exclaimed.

"Well you must be a newcomer to not know about this store," said Mr. Tate.

Steve noticed a newspaper on the counter, just inches away from where he sat. It was the Oak Town Chronicle. The date on the front page of the Chronicle was Tuesday, October 5, 1954.

"This is impossible," he said silently to himself. "This can't be."

"Is that today's paper?" asked Steve.

"Of course it is! What paper do you expect to see?" responded Mr. Tate with a sarcastic voice. "This paper was delivered this morning!"

Steve just stared with a blank look on his face. Mr.

Tate seemed irritated as he didn't understand why they were asking such weird questions.

Mr. Tate, again, proceeded to make two chocolate milkshakes. He, methodically, put two huge scoops of chocolate ice cream in the blender with two cups of milk from a glass container taken from the refrigerator. Steve watched every move by Mr. Tate made and wondered what was going on.

Mr. Tate served the two milkshakes to them and said, "That will be ten cents, boys."

"What?" questioned Joey.

"That will be 10 cents. That's what the sign says!" in a sarcastic voice. Joey stared at him and did not know what to say.

Mr. Tate jovially pointed at the sign located just above the ice cream freezer: SPECIAL TODAY-- MILKSHAKES ONLY 5¢. Joey rubbed his eyes in disbelief. This was simply not real to him.

Joey reached into his pocket to retrieved two nickels and gave it to Mr. Tate.

"Thank you," Joey and Steve said as they left the counter with their milkshakes. They exited the store and sat down on the front porch steps.

"This can't be happening. I don't know why!" Joey exclaimed.

"I don't know what is going on either but I have a feeling it has something to do with the 1954 nickel you found," Steve said.

"No! Don't be silly. It can't be," Joey quickly responded.

Joey reached into his pocket to look at the coin again. He realized that he no longer had it as he frantically searched among the other coins. He must have used it to pay for the milkshakes.

"Oh! No! I gave it to Mr. Tate."

"You did what,"

"I gave the coin to Mr. Tate," Joey repeated.

At that moment, they noticed a cloud of dust trailing behind this approaching car. The car came to a stop at the gas pump. The driver quickly exited and rushed onto the porch. He yelled out to Mr. Tate to come outside and see his new car.

Mr. Tate walked onto the porch as the driver said, "What do you think of my brand new car. It's a 1954 Chevrolet Bel Air. I just bought it today!"

"I love it Greg!" as Mr. Tate walked over to have a closer look. "It is a beauty!"

"I'll take you for a ride later!" Greg said.

"That's a deal. I will meet you in town later today after I close the store."

"Okay. I'll be waiting!" responded Greg.

"Oh, by the way. I want to introduce to you my new friends, Joey and Steve."

"Well, hello boys!" Greg politely said.

Joey and Steve could not respond. The course of events witnessed by Joey and Steve was inescapable.

They left abruptly with no attempt to say goodbye. They quickly grabbed all the gear and the fish with no concern for anything else. The ghastly occurrence was too much for them to handle. Their main concern was to get back home. From the sudden urge to leave, they left their milkshakes on the front porch steps.

Mr. Tate yelled at them as they ran from the store. "Are you not going to finish your milkshake?" Greg was not sure what was going on but ignored the situation.

The trip back home was quick yet seemed like eternity. They took the shortcut through Mr. Coulter's field as they did that morning.

Joey and Steve ran into the house with obvious fear and exhaustion.

"What's going on?" question his mom with deep concern.

Joey, out of breath, attempted to explain but his words just rattled on in a jumbled-up manner.

"Slow down Joey!" his mother shouted.

At that moment, his father walked into the room, startled at what he witnessed. "What is going on Joey?"

Joey tried to explain again but it did not make any sense to anyone. Steve just watched as Joey's parents were irritated at what Joey was saying.

"Slow down Joey! Take a deep breath and calm down!" his dad sternly insisted.

"Dad, we were walking home down Oak Alley Road when suddenly we came upon an old grocery store. We have never seen this before. It wasn't there when we went fishing this morning and now it is there!"

"Son, there is no grocery store down that road. That road is an old logging road leading to Cypress Pond. I have walked down that road many times and it dead-ends at the bend. You must be mistaken," exclaimed his dad. "Remember when you and I went fishing at Cypress Pond a couple of weeks ago?"

"Dad, we saw it!" exclaimed Joey. "We even bought two milkshakes from Mr. Tate!"

"It's true," said Steve with a quiver in his voice.

"If you don't believe us, we will take you there!" replied Joey. "Please. Let us take you there!"

"You mentioned Mr. Tate. Who is Mr. Tate?" his dad asked.

"He is the owner of the store. He spoke to us. This truly happened, Dad. He was there. We both saw him. We even walked into the store." Joey was on the verge of tears.

"Well Joey, if it makes you feel any better, let's go!"

Without hesitation, Joey and Steve left the room with his dad following them. They hopped into the car and headed down Oak Alley Road.

Within minutes, they arrived as Joey and Steve pointed nervously toward the presumed area of the grocery store. Nothing was there. They persistently said that this was the spot.

"Dad, I am telling you the truth. It was here. I remember! I am not lying!" Joey exclaimed.

Steve agreed. "It was here! Where is it? Where is it?" he asked loudly.

They all got out of the car and looked around. They searched and searched for any clue or sign of the store's existence. Joey's dad witnessed the frantic search for something that didn't exist. He remained silent as the boys roamed vigorously from one place to another with no result.

Suddenly, Steve noticed two milkshake glasses near an old cypress log. "Hey, I found something."

Joey rushed over as Steve picked them both up. It resembled the glasses used by Mr. Tate for their milkshakes. They also noticed two coins next to the log as well. Joey picked up the coins and to his astonishment, he held the clue they needed.

"Look Dad, one nickel is a 1954 and the other is a 2015," Joey blurted out with joy. "It must be the two coins I used to pay Mr. Tate for our milkshakes." His dad was very leery about what he heard. It was unbelieving in the least.

"And look Dad. These are two milkshake glasses."

"Let's go home," Joey's dad said angrily. He felt that they took him for a ride, literally. He felt used in their youthful pranks and wanted to get back home.

Joey and Steve felt disappointed that they did not find more proof of Tate's Grocery Store. They were also disappointed that Joey's dad didn't believe them. Joey placed both coins back in his pocket as they entered the car with tears in his eyes.

The trip back home was very awkward. For a moment, Joey doubted his own story as well. They both stared out the window in disgust. They could not solve the mystery and they could not convince Joey's dad. What were they to do?

They soon arrived back at home without uttering another word. Joey's dad got out of the car and walked briskly toward the house with a disgusted look on his face. Joey and Steve exited the car with sadness and despair.

Joey reached into his pocket to look at the coin again. He had to convince himself what happened really did happen.

Steve, too, stared at the coin and said, "There must be a way to solve this mystery. Maybe someone could help us!"

Joey thought for a while and, surprisingly, came up with a brilliant idea. "Let's go to the library and research the history of Oak Town. Maybe, we can ask the librarian for help as well."

"Great idea, Joey!" said Steve.

They ran to the library located three blocks from home. It seemed farfetched but they had nothing to lose. They rushed in and went directly to the front desk to meet Ms. Ansor, the librarian. She knew a lot about Oak Town. She had been a resident of the town for fifty years or more. Joey and Steve felt confident that she could help them.

"May I help you boys?" Ms. Ansor asked.

"Yes 'mam. We are interested about the history of Oak Town, especially in the 1950's.

Ms. Ansor was quite amused and excited that Joey and Steve showed interest about the history of Oak Town. She was somewhat intrigued that they specifically wanted the history of the town from the early fifties.

Her expertise in history was known by many of the residents. She once taught history at Oak Town Middle many years ago. She was a dedicated librarian and took her job very seriously. She never hesitated to find answers to questions, particularly about local history.

She sat down at her desk and researched her documents on Oak Town. She archived all of it on her computer and was able to retrieve it quickly. Joey and Steve watched her as she searched one page after another. They patiently waited for Ms. Ansor to find something of value.

"Now, what is it that you are interested in finding out about Oak Town?" she asked.

"We were interested in old grocery stores of the past," Joey exclaimed.

"Well, that is quite interesting. I do remember two

old grocery stores in town. We had one on Main Street called John's All-Town Grocery. Let me think for a second. Oh, yes! We had one called Tate's Grocery out on Oak Alley Road."

"That's it!" Steve blurted out with total excitement.

"Shhhh, not so loud. You are in the library!" said Ms. Ansor.

She researched every document she had and didn't find anything on Tate's Grocery Store. She continued but, to no avail, came up empty-handed.

"I have another idea," she said.

She led them to the Research and Archive Room located toward the back of the library. It was a room that stored old periodicals, books and newspapers of the past. She was very meticulous about the order of things and she made certain that all items in the room were categorically arranged to dates. She knew her materials quite well.

She carefully searched through several stacks of old newspapers with precision. Steve was quite impressed with Ms. Ansor as she persistently searched and finally located an organized pile of old newspapers which dated back to the early fifties.

"Here they are," she said. "You should find something you need in these papers."

She was very strict in stating her library rules of taking care of all materials. They gladly agreed with pleasure. She trusted them in their quest for historical knowledge. She returned to the front desk as Joey and Steve continued their search. They looked at each fragile newspaper with extreme care and caution.

They looked tirelessly for a specific newspaper dated October 5, 1954. Through determination and persistence, Steve found the newspaper.

"Look Joey. I found it!" He recognized the front page of the Oak Town Chronicle. It was just as he remembered it at Tate's Grocery. It was like finding gold in a mine. It was a feeling that was indescribable.

They carefully placed the newspaper on the table nearby. They shook with excitement but still with uncertainty. They turned each page slowly as they search for any possible clue.

There it was; right before their eyes. In total amazement, Steve pointed at the advertisement of Tate's Grocery Store. They even had a picture of the store with Mr. Tate standing on the front porch. At the bottom of the page was the advertisement: SPECIAL TODAY--MILKSHAKES FOR 5¢.

This couldn't have made them happier. Joey and Steve looked at each other with a sigh of relief. The proof they needed was staring right back at them without a question in mind. They unraveled the truth of the past.

They carefully placed all other newspapers back in their proper order. They did not want to disappoint Ms. Ansor. It was the least they could do for her.

Joey brought the newspaper to the counter as Steve followed close behind. "Ms. Ansor! Could you please make a copy of this advertisement for us?" asked Joey.

She politely replied, "Sure. Oh, you found it. There it is; Tate's Grocery Store. I remember going there quite often as a young child. My father used to buy milkshakes for me. Chocolate was my absolute favorite!"

Joey and Steve just looked at each other with a huge grin on their face. She gave them a piece of history that they also experienced. They did not disclose their secret of what happened to them today. It was better left unsaid.

Joey felt that Ms. Ansor had some idea why they needed the picture but he knew that could not be possible. Strange things have happened but that would be too unbelievable.

They waited patiently for the copy of that page.

They were fidgety the whole time. It was an agonizing wait but they knew it would be well-worth it.

Steve uttered silently to Joey, "I still can't believe we found it." Joey was too uptight to respond.

Ms. Ansor finally approached the counter with the copy they requested. She said, "That will be five cents."

Joey reached into his pocket and, this time, made certain that he would not use the coin from 1954. He did not want to let go of this powerful relic. His shaky hands sweated with anxiety. He paid her five cents and they both said "Thank you!"

They left the library with the copy in Joey's hand. It was as valuable as the coin, maybe even more.

"I can't believe we have the proof," Joey said.

"Me too!"

They arrived at Joey's house and gave his dad the copy from the Oak Town Chronicle. "See, Dad! I told you that we were not lying! Now, do you believe us?" asked Joey.

He looked at the photo in amazement. He came to realize that they were telling the truth. The photo showed an historical part of Oak Town that he didn't know existed.

"Wow! I can't believe it," he said.

Now, they must pursue the truth. They left the house determined to solve this mystery once and for all. The trip there was almost too much for Joey and Steve to handle. The nervousness of this whole ordeal had them practically uncontrollable. They wanted to find more clues since they had proof the store existed. They just wanted something besides a coin and milkshake glasses.

Joey's dad seemed very impatient to get down Oak Alley Road. He drove quickly as a cloud of dust trailed behind them.

They could not get there fast enough.

"Look ahead Dad!" Joey screamed with excitement. "There it is. The grocery store is on the left, exactly where we told you it was!"

Joey's dad stared in disbelief. He stopped the car next to the gas pump in front of the store. To his amazement, the sign on the front of the store read OPEN FOR BUSINESS.

They all got out of the car and looked at each other in complete silence. "Dad, I told you we told the truth!" Joey said.

Joey's dad became even more perplexed as he saw that his car was a 1954 Chevrolet Bel Air. It was brand new and polished to a high shine. Mr. Tate walked out of the store and stood on the porch.

"Hi folks," Mr. Tate said. "Nice car. This was the second brand new car I saw today. When did you get it?"

Steve, Joey and his dad just stood there as unlikely bystanders. Joey's dad looked at Mr. Tate as though he saw a ghastly apparition. He simply could not respond to Mr. Tate.

"Are you okay, sir? Mr. Tate asked.

"Uh, yes," he silently responded.

"I guess you boys want another one of my favorite milkshakes?" asked Mr. Tate. "You left in quite a hurry earlier. I did not know what happened."

It took a few seconds for Steve to respond but he did with certainty. "Yes sir, we sure do!" Joey's dad was mute and was struck with terror.

Mr. Tate, again, invited them into his store to get milkshakes. All three walked into the store following Mr. Tate. Joey and Steve walked over to the counter as Joey's dad stood behind them and remained speechless.

"We would like chocolate, please!" said Joey.

"How about you, sir?" asked Mr. Tate.

"Uh, sure! Chocolate." It took every effort possible to respond.

Mr. Tate got several scoops of chocolate ice cream from the freezer and put it into the blender. He poured three cups of milk from the glass milk bottle. Now the sights and sounds were more familiar to Joey and Steve.

A newspaper was at the end of the counter just inches away from Steve. He recognized front page of the Chronicle. He picked it up and handed it to Joey's dad.

"Look! It's true! We told you the truth!" Steve said.

It was the Oak Town Chronicle and it was Tuesday, October 5, 1954.

Mr. Tate handed each one a delicious chocolate milkshake. "That will be five cents." Mr. Tate said.

"What?" questioned Joey's dad.

"That will be five cents. That's what the sign says," Mr. Tate said in a sarcastic voice.

Joey's dad stared at him and didn't know what to say. Mr. Tate jovially pointed at the sign located just above the ice cream freezer: SPECIAL TODAY— MILKSHAKES ONLY 5¢.

Joey's dad rubbed his eyes in disbelief. This was simply not real to him.

He reached into pocket and retrieved a nickel. He gave the nickel to Mr. Tate.

"Boys, this is my treat! No charge today for you both."

They all said "Thank you!"

They left in unison with their milkshakes in hand and sat down on the steps of the porch. Joey and Steve could not believe it. They were all sitting together at Tate's Grocery Store. No doubt in their mind that they were inhabitants of the past.

Joey reached into his pocket and retrieved the 1954 coin. "Dad, I will forever keep this coin."

"Son, I do not blame you. The relic is your key to the past."

The chocolate milkshake was the most delicious milkshake ever.

"This is a taste of the good ole times," Joey's dad said. That was the second milkshake for Joey and Steve that day.

They slurped every drop from their glass. Mr. Tate heard it and smiled immensely.

They walked inside to return the empty glasses and to thank Mr. Tate.

"See you soon!" Mr. Tate said with a great smile.

"You certainly will!" said Steve.

Mr. Tate followed them out of the store with joy. He knew they were satisfied customers. As they approached the car, Mr. Tate smiled and said "Take care of that beautiful car!"

"I sure will! Thanks for everything especially the great milkshake," Joey's dad responded.

"You bet!" he said.

They got into the car and waved to Mr. Tate as they drove away. Joey and Steve stared out the back window with a trail of dust behind them. Mr. Tate smiled as he waved goodbye. It was as though he did not want them to leave and hoped they would return soon. Not a word was spoken. It was a priceless moment in time. It was an unexplainable journey back to the past

They arrived home and got out of the car. To their complete surprise, the car was no longer a 1954 Chevrolet Bel Air. They are now back in the present where they need to be. It is necessary to keep this secret among them. They knew that it is the only right thing to do. They were concerned that no one would believe them, not even for a second.

Joey retrieved the coin from his pocket as they all looked at it again. What began as a fishing trip ended up being a trip back in time.

"Do ya'll want to go fishing tomorrow at Cypress Pond?" asked Joey's dad.

"You bet!" Steve and Joey responded.

THE LETTER

T his unforgettable story in the life of the Neil family was quite mystifying in the least. Their life in Danville, Mississippi was a typical one until the course of events led to the most bizarre and unexplainable reunion.

Danville was a small, friendly town with a population of only 540 people. Everyone was friendly and helpful to each other. It was a wonder that more people did not move to Danville from the big cities nearby.

The hustle and bustle of the townspeople in Danville was an everyday occurrence. Everyone had a job to do or a place to go. With no exception, was the delivery of the mail to each and every home and business.

The Danville Post Office hired a new postman named Mr. Walkman. He replaced Mr. Riley who recently retired after thirty-five years of service. Mr. Riley was well-liked by everyone because of his loyal and friendly disposition.

Mr. Walkman came from a town approximately one hundred fifty miles away called Benton. He lived there until his reassignment to Danville. He did not mind it a bit as it was a welcomed change in his life.

It was his first day on the job as the new postman and he hoped that everyone would be pleased with him. His early morning route was carefully planned to be as efficient as possible. He wanted the mail delivered on time and most importantly to the correct address.

Mr. Walkman knew it was summer break for students of Danville as he saw many of them out and about. He noticed that many students were at Time Park located just minutes from the post office.

Time Park offered many activities for people young and old. It was a place to visit and enjoy the peacefulness and tranquility of the town. It was a safe haven for all.

Johnny, Mary, David and Carrie were best friends who attended Danville Middle School and have been friends since Kindergarten. If you wanted to find them, look no farther than Time Park. It was their usual place of refuge from boredom.

It was 9:30 when David noticed that Mr. Walkman approached his home to deliver the mail. He wanted to be there and introduce himself and his friends.

"Look, our new mailman!" said David. "Let's go meet him."

They all agreed and hurriedly ran to David's house which was just a short distance from Time Park. They arrived in seconds to greet Mr. Walkman before he placed the mail in the mailbox.

"Hi! Do you have mail for me?" asked David.

"Well, I guess I do if you live at 1054 Wright Street," chuckled Mr. Walkman.

"Yes, I do! My name is David and these are my friends, Mary, Johnny and Carrie."

"My name is Mr. Walkman and I am the new postman in town. Well, no need to put the mail in the box if I can give it to you David," he said with a smile.

"Sure, I'll take it and bring it to my mom."

He handed the mail to David and proceeded to the next house on his route.

"I will see you guys later. Have a great day!" he said with a friendly smile.

"You too!" they all responded.

David quickly brought the mail and laid it down on the front porch for his mom to get later.

David and his friends returned to Time Park as they watched Mr. Walkman deliver the mail to other homes nearby.

"He seems like a very nice man," said Carrie.

"Yeah, but I sure do miss Mr. Riley," replied Johnny. "He was so friendly and laughed all the time."

"Mr. Riley always joked around with us and I sure do miss that," said Mary.

"I felt as though I knew him the first moment we met. That is kind of strange, isn't it?" said David.

"Kinda weird, if you ask me," Johnny said with a chuckle.

"I never met Mr. Walkman before today but it sure felt like I did," repeated David. "I can't remember."

"What gave you that idea," Mary asked.

"I don't know. I just don't know!" he said.

David and his friends had a great morning together. They talked about so many things. One of the things David brought up in conversation several times was the odd feeling he had when he met Mr. Walkman. It was on his mind all morning long.

Mrs. Neil realized that David picked up the mail when she sat down in her rocker on the front porch. This was a peaceful place to sit and rest a bit.

She decided to sort through the mail and as usual it contained many bills; however, one piece of mail was quite peculiar. It was an old letter addressed to David Neil.

It was an unusual letter, indeed, as it had a fifteen cent postage stamp. The cost for postage was forty-two cents and it did not have postage due on the envelope. The letter had a return address but it was very faded; therefore, she couldn't read it.

"I wonder who sent this letter," she said to herself.

She just slipped the letter back with the other mail and brought it indoors. She placed the mail on the kitchen table for Mr. Neil to check it when he came home that afternoon.

Later that evening, Mr. Neil looked at the mail and noticed David had a letter. He, too, was puzzled at the condition of the letter.

"David, I have a letter here for you."

David walked into the room excitedly as he seldom was a recipient of any mail. Today was different.

"Who is this letter from?" David said.

"I don't know. Open it David," his mother said curiously.

He opened the envelope and read the letter silently to himself. What he read was mystifying and confusing. It was written by a young boy named J. W. who sent a friendly letter to a close friend named David.

David felt he was reading someone else's mail and it did not make any sense to him at all. Although it was quite interesting, David was baffled.

"This letter can't be for me," David said.

"Well, what's in the letter?" asked his dad.

"I really don't understand. The letter mentioned a class field trip taken, campouts, and several school activities that we participated in. He also thanked me for being a great friend and that he missed me. He was sorry that I had to leave town and he wanted for us to keep in touch. He hoped to visit one day and reminiscence about the fun times we had at school.

"That is so bizarre. Let me see the letter," his mom said.

She looked at the letter with skepticism. There are so many odd things about this which didn't make any sense at all. Again, she mentioned the fact that this letter is old and faded with the incorrect postage on the envelope.

"Dad, this letter is not for me. I don't know anything about what is written," replied David.

"Hey Dear, take a look at this letter! What do think about it?" as she gave the letter to Mr. Neil.

"Yeah, it's rather strange."

"Well, I will give it back to the postman tomorrow. Maybe he can figure it out," she said.

She laid the letter down on the kitchen table as a reminder to give it back to Mr. Walkman. The letter seemed to possess a certain power of attraction that she could not explain.

David called Johnny and told him about the letter he got in the mail. He told him how confused he was with the contents of the letter.

Johnny thought it may have been a prank played on David by someone.

"I don't think so Johnny. It looks authentic to me," replied David.

"What are you going to do with the letter?" asked Johnny.

"Well, Mom will give it to Mr. Walkman tomorrow."

"Let me know what you find out, okay,"

"Okay. I will. I'll see you tomorrow at the park around nine o'clock," as David hung up the phone.

"Mom, can I show my friends tomorrow morning, before you give it to Mr. Walkman?" asked David.

"I guess, but bring it back to me as soon as possible."

The next day, David picked up the letter off the kitchen table and walked to Time Park to meet his friends.

"Look at this letter guys," David said. "It is so strange. I got this in the mail yesterday."

"So, this is the letter you told me about last night," said Johnny.

"Yes! Read it yourself."

Johnny, Mary and Carrie read it silently to themselves. They, too, were confused.

"So, what do you think about the letter?" Carrie asked.

"Well, nothing in it relates to me or anything! And look at the envelope."

"David, do you know J. W.?" asked Carrie.

"No, I don't! I don't know of anyone by that name."

"What are you going to do with it?" asked Mary.

"Yeah, David. What are you going to do with it?" asked Johnny.

"My mother told me to bring it back to her as soon as I can. She said she would give it to Mr. Walkman today," said David. "I need to bring it back to mom, now."

They walked to David's house as quickly as they could. They realized that the mail was already delivered for the day as they saw Mr. Walkman next door.

"Mom! I am back. Here is the letter," David said.

"Mr. Walkman just delivered the mail five minutes ago," she said disappointedly.

"I know. We saw him talking to Mr. Adams next door," said David.

"I don't want to bother him with the letter while he is on his delivery route. I will go to the post office later."

"Mom, I want to bring it to him now. I know he wouldn't mind."

"I guess you're right," she said.

Mrs. Neil, David and his friends quickly left the house to meet Mr. Walkman next door. Fortunately, he was still there, visiting with Mr. Adams.

"Good morning!" she said with a happy greeting.

Mr. Walkman and Mr. Adams responded "Good morning!"

"Oh, and good morning to you and your friends David," Mr. Walkman said in a cheerful voice.

"Good morning to you, too," they said.

"I am so sorry to bother you but I have a letter that I need help with," she said. "We got this letter yesterday which is addressed to my son David and we do not know where it came from. We read the letter and it is not for him.

She gave the letter to Mr. Walkman and said "I hope you can solve this mystery for us."

"I'm sure I will," as he placed it in the side pouch of his mailbag away from the other mail.

"Thank you so much," she said.

"Have a nice day," Mr. Walkman replied.

Mrs. Neil felt that it would not be solved that easily. The letter was obviously an old, lost letter that just got mixed in with other mail by accident. That was her only explanation at the moment. "But why was it sent to David Neil?" she asked herself.

Mrs. Neil walked back home as David left with his friends. David knew that his mom expected him home for lunch.

As David walked with his friends to Time Park, he mentioned again how Mr. Walkman looked familiar.

"I felt it again! I know him from somewhere," David said again. "It is such a weird feeling."

"Mr. Walkman will solve this mystery soon, I'm sure," said Carrie.

It was time for lunch and David said goodbye to his friends and walked home. He arrived home just in time as lunch was served.

"Hi David," his father said. "How was your morning?"

"Hi Dad! I was at the park with my friends," he responded.

"I gave the letter to Mr. Walkman today, Dear," said Mrs. Neil.

"Well, what did he have to say?" Mr. Neil asked.

"Oh, he said he would take care of it. I'm still puzzled about the whole thing."

"Great! I am very curious about that letter," Mr. Neil responded quickly.

"You know Mom and Dad, I felt that Mr. Walkman and I have met before and we know each other, but that is impossible. I only met him yesterday," David said.

"Well, you are absolutely right! That is impossible," his dad responded.

Suddenly, Mrs. Neil heard a loud knock at the front door. She walked over to see who it was and became excited to know it was Mr. Walkman.

She opened the door and greeted him. "Hi! Did you find out any information on the letter?" she asked.

"Mrs. Neil," he said with a shaky voice. "I have something to talk to you about."

"Okay, come on in. We are in the dining room. Would you like some lunch with us?" She responded.

"No! Thank you. But, I have something very important to tell you," he repeated in a concerned voice.

"Alright; wait here while l get Mr. Neil."

Mr. Walkman stood impatiently as he held the letter that Mrs. Neil gave to him that morning. David and his parents walked into the room to greet Mr. Walkman.

"Hi Mr. Walkman. Well, what did you find out about the letter?" Mr. Neil asked.

"Hi to you both," he said. They could tell that Mr. Walkman was deeply troubled.

Mr. Walkman paced nervously back and forth as he gathered enough strength to tell the Neil family what he found out about the letter.

"This letter was sent thirty years ago to this address. It was sent to a young boy named David Neil. What is so mysterious is that this letter was sent by a J.W. from Benton, Mississippi. I know that place very well because I was the one who sent it. I am J.W. and David Neil was my best friend from Benton Middle School."

"What?" They all responded together.

"My name is Justin Walkman. They called me J.W. for short. I sent this letter to this address because this was the home that David and his family moved to when they left Benton."

"A boy with the same name and who lived at the same address? This is too bazaar!" Mrs. Neil responded in disbelief. "Where is your friend living now?" she asked.

"Well, I found out that he later joined the military after he graduated from Danville High School. He died serving our country. His gravesite is here in town."

"I can't believe this," Mr. Neil said.

"This letter was lost somehow and finally arrived at this address thirty years late. I am amazed that your son is also named David Neil and lives at the same address as my long lost friend. This was my first day as the postman in Danville and I just didn't realize what happened until minutes ago," Mr. Walkman said.

He continued to tell them about the letter he sent to his friend David. They all gazed at him in complete silence. His recollection of what was in the letter made him teary-eyed.

"He was my best friend. We did so much together and when he did not respond to my letter, I assumed he moved on with new friends at his new school here in Danville. But in fact, he never got the letter. He must have felt the same way I did; in that I made new friends and forgot about him," he said with a sad voice.

"How could this letter be lost for such a long time?" Mr. Neil asked.

"Not sure, but one thing for certain, it was meant for you to get it and give it back to me. It was destined for me to move to Danville for my reunion with a long lost friend. Fate brought us back to each other in a most strange way," Mr. Walkman responded.

Everyone listened as Mr. Walkman continued to talk about his friend, David. He remembered quite well about the events mentioned in the letter and it brought many fond memories of their friendship.

The mysterious delivery of a long lost letter to a boy of the same name living at the same address was more than they all could comprehend.

To think that Mr. Walkman delivered his letter to his best friend he wrote thirty years ago was simply incredulous.

"I was told by the postmaster that my friend David was buried at Danville Memorial Cemetery. Would you all like to join me to visit him at the cemetery?" asked Mr. Walkman.

"Yes, indeed!" Mr. Neil responded.

"Yes!" David said.

They all left and walked together four blocks to the cemetery. They were all silent as it gave Mr. Walkman time to reflect on his friend and just how unfortunate that he never received the letter.

They walked past Time Park on their trip there. Carrie, John and Mary looked on as they knew David had his answer to his mysterious letter. They, of course, had no knowledge of how extraordinary this all turned out to be.

They arrived at the cemetery and looked tirelessly for the gravesite of Mr. David Neil. They walked down each row and read each name on every headstone to locate him.

"I found him!" David shouted with excitement.

They all rushed to where David stood. Mr. Walkman felt he could not get there quick enough.

"Look everyone! He was Captain David Neil of the United States Army!" David said loudly.

"He served his time to give us all the freedom to live in our great country," Mr. Walkman said.

They all stood together staring at the headstone. They saw his date of death. It was June 10, 2005.

"That was exactly five years ago to this day," said Mr. Walkman. "Just five years ago. I can't believe it. Just five years ago!"

Mr. Neil placed his hand on Mr. Walkman's shoulder as a way to ease the pain. Mrs. Neil had tears in her eyes as she witnessed his grief.

"It was you, David, that brought me back to my best friend," Mr. Walkman said.

David looked at the headstone and said "My name is David Neil, also. I just received your letter that you never got from your best friend Mr. Walkman or J.W. as you called him."

David opened the envelope and read it aloud for all to hear, but more importantly, for Captain David Neil.

J.W. was glad David read the letter. He knew that it would have been very difficult for him to do. When David finished, Mr. Walkman stood erect and saluted his best friend, Captain David Neil.

"I am so sorry you did not get the letter sent thirty years ago. I sure do miss you as my best friend. Thanks for getting me here to meet another David Neil. Now I know why I felt I knew him the first time we met. How strange is that!" Mr. Walkman said.

"I felt the same way when I met you at the mailbox yesterday Mr. Walkman."

David reverently laid the letter on top of the grave. The letter was finally delivered to the right person. Unfortunately it was the wrong address. He no longer lived at 1054 Wright Street in Danville, Mississippi.

Printed in the United States
By Bookmasters